LITTLE MISS NAUGHTY

and the Good Fairy

Roger Hargreaves

Original concept by
Roger Hargreaves

Written and illustrated by
Adam Hargreaves

EGMONT

Little Miss Naughty got up, stretched, opened her curtains and looked out of her window.

"What's that?" she said, peering more closely.

She went downstairs, out of the back door and down to the bottom of her garden.

"Look at that!" she cried. "It's a Fairy ring!"

On the ground at her feet was a ring of mushrooms growing in the dewy grass.

"I wonder what happens if I step into the ring?" thought Little Miss Naughty out loud.

So she did.

And what happened was that she shrank to the size of a matchbox.

Which surprised her enormously.

"Oh help!" she wailed. "What do I do now?"

She looked around the Fairy ring and noticed that there was a door in the stem of one of the mushrooms.

"I wonder what happens if I go through that door?" she asked herself.

So she did.

And what happened was that she found herself in a quite different world.

Fairyland!

Little Miss Naughty stepped out into a beautiful, magical wood. On a hilltop in the distance was a glittering castle. Little Miss Naughty set off to see who lived there.

"Who are you?" asked a voice above her.

Startled, Little Miss Naughty looked up to find a Fairy with gossamer wings hovering just above her head.

"I'm Little Miss Good," lied Little Miss Naughty.

"What a coincidence! I'm the Good Fairy. You must come and stay the night."

The Good Fairy waved her magic wand and whisked them up to her castle.

And it was the Good Fairy's magic wand that captured Little Miss Naughty's attention all evening long.

Little Miss Naughty could think of nothing but the mischief she might get up to if she was a Fairy with her own magic wand and her own wings.

That night Little Miss Naughty was very naughty.

She stole the Good Fairy's wand!

She crept out of the castle and ran all the way back to the magical wood where she had entered Fairyland. There she found a door in a tree which opened into the ring of mushrooms at the bottom of her garden.

As soon as she stepped out of the Fairy ring she grew back to her normal size.

Once Little Miss Naughty was safely inside her house she looked at the wand in her trembling hand.

She closed her eyes and waved the wand and at the same time she said, "Turn me into a Fairy."

When she opened her eyes and looked in the mirror she saw she had a perfect pair of Fairy wings.

She gave them a little flutter and felt herself rise off the floor.

"Oh what fun!" she cried. "Oh, what fun I am going to have!"

The next day, flying along above the rooftops she saw Mr Bump walking along the pavement.

She waved the magic wand and a hole appeared in front of Mr Bump and in he fell.

From her perch on a chimney pot high above, Little Miss Naughty chuckled to herself.

But at that very moment a high wall fell across the pavement just where Mr Bump would have been walking if he hadn't fallen into the hole.

"Thank goodness I fell into this hole," said Mr Bump, peering up the street.

Little Miss Naughty flew out across the countryside where she found Farmer Barns looking at his field of corn.

With another chuckle, Little Miss Naughty waved the wand and the field of corn turned into a ploughed field.

But there in the middle of the field was the farmer's dog who had been lost amongst the corn.

"Thank goodness the corn disappeared and I have found Fido," said a relieved Farmer Barns.

Little Miss Naughty was very puzzled.

It seemed that as hard as she tried to be naughty, things kept turning out for the best.

She made it rain on Little Miss Sunshine, who could not have been happier because her tomatoes needed watering.

She created a mess in Little Miss Neat's front room and Little Miss Neat was overjoyed because she had Mr Messy coming for tea later that day and she wanted to make him feel at home.

By the time Little Miss Naughty got home she had never caused so much happiness in her life.

She was miserable.

"This thing's no good," she said, throwing the wand down on the table.

"That is where you are very wrong" said a voice.

Little Miss Naughty nearly jumped out of her skin.

It was the Good Fairy.

"That wand is all good because it is my wand. I hope that making so many people happy may have done *you* some good."

"So this wand will only make good things happen?" asked Little Miss Naughty.

"That's right."

"And this wand will never allow you to do anything naughty?"

"That's right."

"There is one more thing I need to know," said Little Miss Naughty.

"What is that?" asked the Good Fairy.

"Where does the Naughty Fairy live?"